DEDICATIONS

I was very active in the school and library communities of Newtown and Sandy Hook, Connecticut, where I lived with my family for thirty-five years. My first book for children was published just before we moved there, and was followed by a hundred more books that were created in the attic studio of our old farmhouse. The changing seasons in the woodlands, fields, and streams that surround the Sandy Hook village provided an idyllic environment for raising a family. Those scenes and memories inspired these illustrations.

It is my hope that this book celebrates the laughter, the playful high spirits, and the uniqueness of the children of Sandy Hook and of children everywhere.

—STEVEN KELLOGG

I wrote *Snowflakes Fall* after Steven told me of his sadness and concern for his community and for children everywhere. This is a sadness that the world felt, and that I felt too. What brought us comfort was the idea of renewal and memory, and while writing *Snowflakes Fall*, I thought about all children and families affected by loss.

—PATRICIA MACLACHLAN

In honor of the community of Sandy Hook and Newtown, Connecticut, Random House Children's Books has made a donation to the Sandy Hook School Support Fund. This donation, as well as a book donation to the national literacy organization First Book, in support of children everywhere, was made in conjunction with the publication of *Snowflakes Fall*.

Visit us on the Web! randomhouse.com/kids
Educators and librarians, for a variety of teaching tools, visit us at RHTeachersLibrarians.com

Library of Congress Cataloging-in-Publication Data
MacLachlan, Patricia.
Snowflakes fall / by Patricia MacLachlan; illustrated by Steven Kellogg. — First edition. p. cm.
Summary: In this illustrated poem in honor of the victims of the 2012 shooting in Newtown, Connecticut, falling snowflakes celebrate the uniqueness of life, its precious, simple moments, and the strength of memory.
ISBN 978-0-385-37693-8 (trade) — ISBN 978-0-375-97328-4 (lib. bdg.) — ISBN 978-0-375-98219-4 (ebook)
[1. Snow—Fiction.] I. Kellogg, Steven, illustrator. II. Title.
PZ7.M2225Sn 2013 [E]—dc23 2013008622

Book design by John Sazaklis
MANUFACTURED IN CHINA
10 9 8 7 6 5 4 3 2 1

PATRICIA MacLachlan

STEVEN Kellogg

Snowflakes
Fall

RANDOM HOUSE NEW YORK

After the flowers are gone
Snowflakes fall.

Flake

After flake

After flake

Each one a pattern
All its own—
No two the same—
All beautiful.

Snowflakes fall

To sit on gardens

And evergreen trees

On the fur of dogs
And the tongues of laughing children—
No two the same—
All beautiful.

Snowflakes

Fall

Drift

And swirl together

Like the voices of children.

Snowflakes fall
On a winding river's sandy banks

On a hilltop town
On its ancient church
On its loved library
And its familiar flagpole.

When snowflakes fall at night

Wailing winds may blow
And frantic, icy snowflakes
scratch the window glass.

Branches fly
And shadows
darken dreams.

But then—when we wake in the morning light—

Surprise!

The world shines.

Snowflakes fall
To quilt meadows
So we see the wandering prints
Of birds
Rabbits

The bobcat at dawn

And the footprints of small red boots—

Making sled paths

And snowmen

And forts

And fields of snow angels.

And when the snowflakes melt
In quiet sun

They fill the chattering streams

Flowing
Rushing
Sending drops of water up
To fall as rain

On places where the snowflakes had been.

Where soon
Flowers will grow
Again.

And when the flowers bloom
The children remember the snowflakes

And we remember the children—

No two the same—
All beautiful.